T0146907

ANUNNAKI

GODS OF EARTH
AND
NIBIRU

SONNY RAMIREZ

ANUNNAKI GODS OF EARTH AND NIBIRU

iUniverse books may be ordered through booksellers or by contacting:

iUniverse
1663 Liberty Drive
Bloomington, IN 47403
www.iuniverse.com
1-800-Authors (1-800-288-4677)

Because of the dynamic nature of the Internet, any web addresses or links contained in this book may have changed since publication and may no longer be valid. The views expressed in this work are solely those of the author and do not necessarily reflect the views of the publisher, and the publisher hereby disclaims any responsibility for them.

Any people depicted in stock imagery provided by Thinkstock are models, and such images are being used for illustrative purposes only. Certain stock imagery © Thinkstock.

ISBN: 978-1-5320-2694-2 (sc)
ISBN: 978-1-5320-2693-5 (e)

Library of Congress Control Number: 2017913702

Print information available on the last page.

iUniverse rev. date: 09/12/2017

To my brother, Geovanny. He's already in the heavens, waiting for me. After I die, and definitely before I return in my next life, we will soar with the stars. My body, this flesh, will no longer hold me down; it will no longer be my anchor. There will be nothing to hold me down. My brother and I will dance with the universe, and we will hold hands with the galaxies, finally free until we see each other again. I love you to the ends of the universe and back!

INTRODUCTION

I find myself writing this book because of my passion and love for world history, ancient history, ancient civilizations, mythology, the what-ifs, and the what can be. I also ponder on the questions that all humankind has been trying to answer for thousands of years: Is there a God? Where do we come from? Is there life somewhere else? Are we alone? Who made us? Is there an afterlife? Is there a hell?

I drown myself with book after book, reading about different theories, gods, religions, and ancient texts and tablets found and translated by people who have dedicated their lives to giving us answers. I truly admire and respect the work these scholars do. There are many books written by doctors, archaeologists, priests, scientists, former military people, and your ancient alien theorists. I can't get enough of them. I also share my passion with friends and family, and I speak about what I read, what I watch, and new discoveries that fascinate me. I have recommended books, and I've let friends borrow my prized possessions in order to not only teach but also open their minds to a whole new world. The problem is they return the books because they cannot understand them; they are too complicated, or they have too many scientific words and city names without explanation.

For example, if I use the word *khemet* (or *kemet*, depending on whose translation you are reading), it means black land or land of the black people. Some think it is a reference to the Nile, not a description of ethnicity. When speaking of an ancient city, most people don't know I am speaking of what is now Egypt. This book is dedicated to the curious who want to know but do not want to feel like fools for not understanding the full stories or terms. They should not give up on something that will be great! I hated when my friends would get discouraged. I also would read a chapter twice or whole books twice. I'd look up maps, and I still look up words or meanings to better understand them. My love for ancient history is what drives me to learn. I was inspired by my friend, an eleven-year-old who loves history and mythology, Yesenia. I sought to write a book for the first time—the curios, or the starter book if you will.

THE GODS

Names to Remember

Anu (An): Sky Father, King of Gods, King of Heaven, Lord of the Constellations. Anu is married to half sister Antu. The city dedicated to Anu was Uruk, or the biblical city of Erech. Anu's throne is the place of the assembly of the gods. Enlil sits to his right, and Enki sits to the left of Anu at the assembly of the gods. Anu is the father of the gods here on earth and Nibiru. Anu's symbol is the eight-pointed star. His temple in Uruk is known as E. Anna, or House of An. It is believed he fathered eighty children, with fourteen by Antu, his queen.

Enki (Ea): Prince of Eridu; Lord of Earth; deity of crafts, science, knowledge, creation, and the waters; son of Anu. Married to Ninki/ Damkina. Older half brother of Enlil and Ninmah, by different mothers.

Enlil (Hu): Guardian, Lord of Command, Lord of Air, son of Anu. Next in line to take supreme command; legal heir to Anu. Younger half brother of Enki and half brother of Ninmah, who is also his wife.

Ninmah (Ninhursag): Lady of Life, fertility goddess, head scientist of life and genetics, daughter of Anu, half sister by different mothers to Enki and Enlil.

There are many more to name, but these will be the main characters.

THE DISCOVERY

In 1845, Sir Austen Henry Layard and his team were making excavations in ancient Calah (Tel Nimrud). Layard was an English archaeologist, author, art historian, cuneiformist, and politician, among many other things. One would say he was a brilliant man. He is best known for his excavations of Nineveh (on the northern end of today's Mosul, Iraq) and Nimrud (south of Nineveh, also known as Calah in biblical times). He discovered a large amount of the Assyrian Palace Reliefs known today, and in 1847 he discovered and excavated the ancient Assyrian ruins, the Library of Ashurbanipal. He is credited with the discovery of about twenty-two thousand clay texts. Thousands and thousands of years of history were preserved under the desert sands.

He published many important books, such as *Nineveh and Its Remains, Discoveries in the Ruins of Nineveh and Babylon, A Second Series of Monuments of Nineveh*, and *A Popular Account of Discoveries of Nineveh*. Many more books followed. He is credited with identifying Kuyunjik as the site of Nineveh. He would lay down the foundation for future archaeologists, researchers, scholars, and ancient alien theorists.

One very important discovery during the excavations was that they found a series of cuneiform tablets known as the Enuma Elish, best known as the Seven Tablets of Creation. These tablets tell us how the universe came into being, the creation of the world and humanity, and the struggle among the gods. We also learn about the Anunnaki from them. According to numerous researchers, the tablets tell us the story about the gods called the Anunnaki, who came from the heavens to create the human race.

In 1880 George Smith, an English Assyriologist, cuneiformist, and explorer, published *The Chaldean Account of Genesis*. He is mostly

Sumerian Temple (Restored) in the Ancient City of Ur

known for the discovery of the account of the Great Flood, with obvious biblical parallels in 1872. He presents numerous translations from tablets, including the discovery and translation of the Epic of Gilgamesh (Idzubar), the Descent of Ishtar, and the Great Flood.

He also published other great books: *Assyrian Discoveries: An Account of Explorations* and *Discoveries on the Site of Nineveh.*

In 1871 he published *Annals of Assur-bani-pal* and a few other books.

George Smith died at the young age of thirty-six, but with his short time on earth, he left us with great books of his discoveries and translations.

It wouldn't be until 1976 that the Great Zecharia Sitchin published his book *The 12ᵗʰ Planet (The Earth Chronicles).* This is where we get a deeper translation, no-holds-barred. Some say it's the truth, and others disclaim his thirty-plus years of work and research. Mainstream scholars stick to the same story time after time, scared to think outside the box. Once you have been taught to think this, fear this, and love this, you think, "This is how it is. This is how it was." Many people don't think for themselves in order to belong, to not get fired, and to not be ridiculed by their peers. Sometimes the truth can be a scary thing, especially if it can change everything you were told to believe. Many ancient cultures around the world speak of the "star people," Gods that came from the heavens and created life on earth. This story is one of them.

Located at the site of modern Tell el-Muqayyar in southern Iraq, the temple is dated to 6500–3800 BC. Most of the site had been restored, but due to many recent wars in that area of the world, many ancient buildings have been destroyed. At one point it was a beautiful city. The first Hebrew patriarch, Abraham, is believed to have been born in this city. The first inscribed texts and the first cylinder seals were found here. Schoolhouses were found, along with chariots, jewelry made of gold, and court records. Later, it was discovered with great erosion underneath, and the debate began. Some believe it was built before the Great Flood. If that is the case, this temple would be a bit over thirteen thousand years old.

Archaeological excavations have substantiated that early on, Ur possessed great wealth. In 1625 Pietro della Valle excavated the city and recorded the presence of ancient bricks with strange, unknown symbols. With excavations done from 1922 to 1934 by Sir Charles Leonard Woolley, almost 1,850 burials were discovered, 16 of which were considered to be royal tombs. Nanna (Sin), the moon god, was the patron god of Ur. We will compare this temple to others worldwide later.

ANUNNAKI FOR BEGINNERS

Imagine the earth 450,000 years ago. While looking at the sky, you hear a thunderous sound, and the sky opens. A spaceship enters earth's atmosphere. The ship lands on a new planet—Ki is what the Anunnaki called it. They were intergalactic space travelers.

They set up their first alien base, In Eridu (the real Eden, some argue), in southern Mesopotamia (today's Abu Shahrein, Iraq). Their mission was to explore what resources they could use to take back to their home planet, Nibiru. Nibiru is a gigantic planet three to four times bigger than earth, but it does orbit in our solar system. It orbits close to earth every 3,600 years. They were on a mission to search for gold, and a lot of it. They needed it to save the dying atmosphere on their home planet. If they failed, it would be the end of life on Nibiru.

First, the leaders of Nibiru sent a fleet of Anunnaki (it is believed that the Anunnaki were also known as the biblical Nefilim) to explore and make sure everything would be habitable for them. They found it livable, with an atmosphere they could live in, and of course they found the resources they could use. The leaders of the mission contacted the leaders of Nibiru, and Anu sent Enki (the interesting thing is that Anu existed in Sumerian cosmogony as a dome that covered the flat earth; outside of this dome was the primordial body of water known as Nammu) and more Anunnaki. They set up their station, the first city on Earth, Eridu. The city dedicated to Enki, now known as Abu Shahrein, Iraq, is also known as the home of the gods. It was the first city of earth, the first city of the gods. Four more cities on earth would follow to mine the gold in (ancient Mesopotamia: Bad-Tibira, Larak, Sippar, and Shuruppak). These cities were more like mission control centers, and they were where some of the

Anunnaki leaders would call home while they finished their missions on earth.

And so it began. In order to extract the gold, mines had to be established. A lot of them were set up in what is now South Africa. The travel from cities to the mining areas and back was no big deal for the Anunnaki; they had smaller spaceships to travel back and forth. Everything was going good. Gold was being shipped to Nibiru while Nibiru was still close in orbit. Once it was too far from earth, they would store and wait another 3,600 years to send the next shipments. Anu sent Enlil to watch over the whole operation and to be commander of everything going on. Enlil and Enki were the first two leaders of earth. Enlil was the younger brother of Enki, but he alone was the legal heir to become the next leader, the god-king of Nibiru and the true heir to Anu.

They were here about one hundred thousand years. The Anunnaki were getting tired of the hard work they had to endure day to day—this was beneath them, and this is not the work for them. You have to remember they were superior beings, standing ten to twelve feet tall, with some even reaching seventeen feet. They were intelligent, strong space travelers. They were not happy.

The Anunnaki formed an alliance with each other to protest and fight against Enlil and the other commanders of earth, if need be. Something had to change; something needed to be done. They were not working the mines anymore. They protested in front of Enlil's palace. Enlil was never in real danger, but this was a betrayal. One didn't do this to the future king!

Enlil reached out to his father, Anu, to tell him what was going on. He wanted justice for those who opposed him, betrayed him, and dared to double-cross him and the mission. He wanted their deaths! He wanted this nonsense to stop immediately.

Anu set up a council with all the leaders at the Assembly of the Gods. Commanders, scientists, and leaders were at the assembly to see what could be done to continue with the mission as soon as possible. Some suggested more Anunnaki. It was Enki who said, "Let us make a slave, a worker. We shall call him man. We will create a being to do the labor, a slave to take over the yoke of the Anunnaki. Let us make man in our image, in our likeness." The assembly agreed.

It is unclear exactly what the Annunaki looked like. There are depictions

on tablets and stones with a lot of facial hair that hide their faces. They wore wrist bands that look a lot like watches, and they held a conelike object. There were elongated heads in some, and they held a small bag of some sort. There is no real explanation for it; it is definitely one of the most mysterious objects depicted on walls, texts, temples, and ancient cities. One sees this bag not only in ancient Mesopotamia but also around the globe, in all around ancient cultures. What's the connection? What is inside? What does it represent? There are many different theories, and some suggest it represents a bag with the seed of life inside it. Is it ancient alien technology?

Some pictures make them look like man, but with wings. They are holding lions. Even Gilgamesh from the Epic of Gilgamesh is considered half Anunnaki, half human. The lion looks the same size as a person holding a kitten. Some pictures show them with wings like an angel and with the head of an eagle. The wings suggest that they can fly or take flight at any time—a superior being. They were angelic beings, and maybe they could change shapes. The Anunnaki were those of royal blood, those who came from heaven to earth.

It was up to Enki and Ninmah to create this being. They went back to their scientific lab, Edin, where they collected animals and primates that lived on earth. They would experiment and determine which ones would be of use to them. It is suggested that this was the biblical Garden of Eden. They experimented on different subjects and mixed one species with another. There were many failed experiments, many weird and scary creatures. Nothing was to their expectations. This might explain why we have so many depictions around the globe with animal heads, human bodies, three- or four-headed animals, human heads with animal bodies, and two or three animals mixed together. Time was not on their side; they had already been here over one hundred thousand years. The Anunnaki do not age as we do. One year (known as a shar, which means a perfect circle or full circle; it also represents the number 3,600) would be 3,600 years for us. This is one example of how they would be gods: their life span is amazingly superior to a human's. They could live for thousands of years.

Time went by until they found the perfect test subject: an ape-man, an advanced monkey: Australopithecus. Australopithecus was known as a hominid with both apelike and human characteristics. Fossils have been

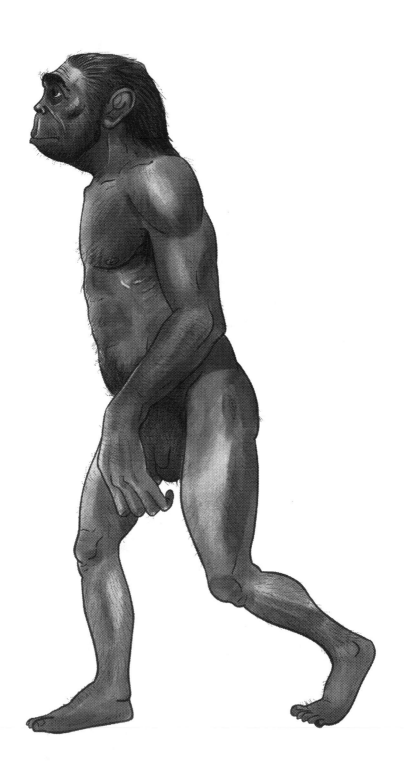

found in eastern and southern Africa. It is considered to have had a small brain, and it lived anywhere between one to four million years ago. It had Long arms, walked upright, was hairy, and had facial features that were more apelike than human. But it was evolving. The ape-man walked the earth long before Homo erectus and Homo sapiens (humans).

Enki and Ninmah started to experiment, trying to make the perfect slave that could do the work. This new being was worked hard, listened to orders, and was very dumb in a sense. There was one problem: the new being could not procreate. It could not have children! It was getting harder and harder for Enki and Ninmah to keep up with the gold demand, and there were not enough ape-men slaves for the workload, so they kept trying.

Finally, Enki and Ninmah decided to put their own DNA in an ape-woman to carry the new man.' They used their own DNA, their own genes, to make a genetically engineered being. It would be the seed of an Anunnaki god, Enki. There are discovered seals that show the goddess Ninmah sitting down and holding a baby next to the tree of life. They called the engineered being Adamu. Adamu was something they were proud of because he was smart, strong, and listened to orders. He would be what the Anunnaki would call perfect.

Now all they needed was a female. She would not be made from his ribs. Other Anunnaki female scientist or volunteers would be pregnant at the same time with the same seed. They would make multiple babies, up to seven boys and seven girls. Ninki, Enki's wife, and the other female Anunnaki would carry the injected seed of Adamu. Seven males and seven females were to be born. With the blood of an Anunnaki god, they created the DNA of Adamu.

Now we go back 300,000 years ago. Ten long months would go by. Finally there was a female born who could procreate, and her name was Tiamat (Eve). Adamu and Tiamat were perfect in the eyes of Enki and Ninmah. They had their perfect being, intelligent, hairless, clear skin, ability to speak, and with the power to procreate. The first Homo sapiens, the first humans!

In the beginning of Homo sapiens, they did not worship a god or gods—they worked for them. (Now, we see Homo sapiens showing up in our history some 250,000 years ago.) The Anunnaki let them work in the garden, took notes, and made sure the slaves followed the rules. Homo sapiens were told by Enlil to take care of the garden, and to never eat the fruit from the Tree of Knowledge. They would be destroyed if they dared break the rule.

It's almost as if they wanted them smart but not too smart, as well as obedient. They wanted hard workers. Do not eat of the Tree of Knowledge. Why? Maybe this was why Enki is portrayed as a serpent in some depictions. We have to remember what history teaches us, and it is that the winner writes history. Maybe Enlil later had Enki represented as a serpent as a betrayal gesture that he was a snake who went against the Anunnaki and protected his creation, the slaves. Enki loved what he had created. It was Enki who told Tiamat/Eve that she would not die from eating from the Tree of Knowledge.

Once more, humans were multiplying they were taught how to talk, grow vegetables, hunt, mine the gold, domesticate animals for food, and perform all the labors that the Anunnaki were in charge of doing. They also started to reproduce. After all, that was what it was about: the perfect hard-working, obedient slave. A new world begins for man, but as easily disposable slaves.

That is my understanding on the creation of man. Could it be that fantastic of a history? The theories seem more like a Hollywood sci-fi movie. Always more questions than answers. I love history!

About 250,000 years ago, the Anunnaki had been here for 180,000 years. Mainstream scholars argue the point on how we came from Homo erectus to Homo sapiens so quickly. Evolution doesn't move that fast. How did this happen almost overnight? There is no history to tell us, no true explanation how we were Home erectus. Then there was a big bang: boom—we are Homo sapiens. We were creating civilizations, building gigantic monuments, creating laws, learning astronomy, writing, creating religions, and so on. Somehow, they want us to believe we were simply monkeys. With a rope, no wheel, and a sharp rock tied to a stick, somehow the ancients built empires! The Anunnaki did not create us from nothing. They were not our God, not our original creator. What they did was use what was already here, evolving and put in their DNA. They biologically engineered a species, upgraded, and implanted their own image and likeness on Homo sapiens. They helped us evolve to what we are today through hundreds of thousands of years, maybe even millions of years. They hurried up the process.

Too this day, scientists cannot explain our whole DNA. They call it junk DNA. How is my DNA junk? Why can scientists not explain it?

According to a paper published March 21, 2016 By PNAS (Proceedings of the National Academy of Sciences), 8 percent of our DNA is "alien" and is made up of nonhuman viral fragments. The study is "Discovery of Unfixed Endogenous Retrovirus Insertions in Diverse Human Populations." The study came from the Department of Human Genetics, University of Michigan, and the Department of Molecular Biology and Microbiology, Tufts University School of Medicine.

After they studied 2,500 people, they discovered that our DNA is less human and that 19 pieces of ancient viral DNA exist in our own genome.

On the bottom of the paper, it says this.

> Significance: The human endogenous retrovirus (HERV)group HERV-K contains nearly intact and insertionally polymorphic integrations among humans, many of which code for viral proteins. Expression of such HERV-K proviruses occurs in tissues associated with cancers and autoimmune diseases, and in HIV-infected individuals, suggesting possible pathogenic effects. Proper Characterization of these elements necessitates the discrimination of HERV-K loci; such studies are hampered by our incomplete catalog of HERV-K insertions, motivating the identification of additional HERV-K copies in humans. By examining 2,500 sequenced genomes, we discovered 19 previously unidentified HERV-K insertions, including an intact provirus without apparent substitutions that would alter viral function, only the second such provirus described. Our results provide a basis for future studies of HERV evolution and implication for disease.[1]

---

[1] www.pnas.org/content/113/16/E2326.full.pdf

This study has shown us that some people carry insertions that we can't map back to the reference, said coauthor Julia Wildchutte from Tufts University. Basically, it says they still cannot identify out whole DNA; it's as mysterious as ever. Where did that small percentage of DNA come from? And why has it confused scientists to this day? Or do they know and are forbidden to tell us?

The junk DNA provides too many mysteries in our own DNA. Will they ever solve it? Or do they know but refuse to let people know because it might cause chaos? Will religion crumble if such a discovery was made? We are related to the chimpanzee by 96–98 percent of our DNA, but that 2 percent makes us hairless and intelligent enough to make machines to help us fly and drive, learn different languages, read, and more.

On October 20, 2016, the American Society of Human Genetics held its annual meeting. The conclusion they reached was that certain people from Melanesia (an area in the South Pacific that encloses Papua New Guinea and it's neighboring islands) may have some strange genes in their DNA. They believe that the unrecognized DNA belongs to a previously undiscovered species of humanoids. According to Ryan Bohlender, one of the researchers involved in the study, they believe that the species is not Neanderthal or Denisovan. Bohlender stated, "We are missing a population or misunderstanding something about the relationships. With assumptions about population size and more recent population separation dates taken from literature, we estimate the archaic-modern separation date at 440,000 + 300 years ago for all modern human populations. Wow! Another great coincidence: about 440,000 years ago!

Why does it seem like we are a human race with a loss of memory? We know nothing of our real history. Are the governments hiding our real history for national security reasons or their own interests? Are they keeping us in the dark to protect us? Is someone or a society of secret keepers making money by keeping us in the dark? Are the churches hiding it for their own agenda? Are we alien or part alien? Why can we not remember our history, our origin?

And if there was an alien presence that came to earth long ago, what if other alien life found out about the discovery and set their paths to earth too? What's to stop them? And if they did, are they still among us? How about alien abductions, which are still reported today? Are those all made-up lies by millions of people worldwide? Hundreds of myths, stories, and ancient religious beliefs around the world start with "From the heavens, they came." Who are they?

This is why Zecharia Sitchin's work is incredibly provocative and enticing. It's highly important to finding out our real past, our real history, based on the premise that mythology is not fanciful but is the repository of ancient memories. Some tell us we came from monkeys, but we simply cannot evolve from being a monkey, lose our body hair, and then kill a bear or deer for fur to keep warm basically almost overnight. Evolution simply does not work like that.

If God, the father of Jesus, made us, then why are there so many contradictions in the Bible? First it says "Let us make man in our image." Who is *our*? Why is his story almost identical to the story of Horus, son of Osiris and Isis, the great gods of Egypt? Yet the story of Horus was written 2,500–3,500 years before Jesus walked the earth. Regarding the story of Noah, we later find out the ancient Sumerians had an almost identical story written thousands of years before the Bible.

Who built the Great Pyramids of Egypt? Man today cannot pick up some of the stones, some weighing in the access of over eighty thousand tons. Over two million stones were perfectly put together one on top of another. Some suggest it took over twenty years to put together. Impossible!

These are questions we must ask. What if we have been here with civilizations more than one hundred thousand years ago? What if we did have technology, whether our own or alien? The ancient people (our ancestors) were far more advanced then what we are told. The question is, what happened? Where did all the people go? Many cultures, civilizations, and people disappeared, vanished. They left temples, pyramids, and cities all around the globe, vanishing into thin air. Were they taken somewhere? Could some of our ancestors been taken to Nibiru, to be slaves for the Anunnaki on their home planet? Was there a different catastrophe that we are not aware of besides the last one, the Great Flood?

The real truth is we need a miracle or a great discovery that will tell us more. When will we be able to tell the difference between the myth, the story, and the reality of what is translated from Sumerian texts? First, are we ready for the truth? Are we satisfied with the lies? The clay tablets we've found have a very important, incredibly valuable importance in our historical stories, myths—whatever you want to call it. It is always better to be informed than opinionated. We must take them seriously. It does seem that some translations have somehow been misunderstood or poorly translated by mainstream scholars. Ask yourself why. Have they been put on the side until something else is considered a great discovery, to fit their agenda? Let's say it was properly translated and was a new discovery, a new history. What reality would be accepted by mainstream scholars?

Speaking of new discoveries, on January 4, 2017, the *Washington Post* came out with a very interesting article written by Sarah Kaplan: "Mysterious Radio Burst Came from a Galaxy 2.5 Billion Light Years Away, Astronomers Discover." Let me share with you this fantastic news. I suggest you Google this information' I cannot write the whole report here, but I strongly suggest you look it up. There are very fascinating things going on in our galaxy. Scientists have finally found a source of fast radio bursts (FRBs) in a dwarf galaxy 2.5 billion light-years from earth. It is sending out mysterious millisecond radio waves, researchers reported in *Nature* and *Astrophysical Journal Letters*. FRBs are extremely brief pulses of radio waves flaring with the power of about 500 million suns. Scientists have recorded just 18 of these signals, but there have been studies that suggest there could be as many as 10,000 a day. Some researchers believe they must originate in our own galaxy. Researchers looking at archival data from Arecibo Observatory, one of the largest radio telescopes in the world, did find evidence that the bursts were repeatedly coming from the same direction. The signal, called FRB 121102, was definitely repeating, and it certainly traveled a long way to reach earth. Their scan of the sky revealed that FRB 121102's source is 2.5 billion light-years away, within a dwarf galaxy with 1 percent of the mass of the Milky Way. The scientists tell us it could be a million different things causing these radio bursts; they repeat themselves over and over. These FRBs are traveling billions of light-years to us to earth, and yet not even one scientist suggests this could be a signal to reach us. Maybe it can be alien life.

Basically, scientists land on something, and it seems like they got cold feet. There was not one mention that there could be intelligent life sending these radio waves to us. In a little over eighty hours of observation time over a six-month period in 2016, the VLA detected nine bursts from

FRB 121102. The team's observations also revealed an ongoing, persistent source of weaker radio emissions in the region, yet there's no mention of SETI, the Search for Extraterrestrial Intelligence. Where is SETI in all of this? They seem desperate to find a natural explanation for this phenomenon—something more complex than quasars, but not intelligent. We've had decades of searching for something, and as soon as something turns up, they want to tell us it's something else. It could be a million things, but not intelligent life? They're looking out for a million different possibilities, but they're not looking for intelligent life.

I was truly amazed when I read this article. "Wow!" was my first reaction. Did they get cold feet when the possibility of actually contacting another world was a real thought? Are they telling us everything they know? Or is it something bigger than we are led to believe? Only time will tell. This is what I meant when I said, "What reality is okay for scientists, scholars, and archaeologists to share with us?" Is what they tell us 100 percent the truth, or do we get only bits. Maybe what we should start doing is read the Bible literally, as a historical, scientific document. Maybe then we will learn something new that we haven't thought of.

When I was a kid, Mars was dry, too hot in the day, and frozen at night. There was no way life could live there. Now, we know there is water in Mars, there was water a billion years ago, and it's frozen to this day. At one moment in time, it had oceans, rivers, and an atmosphere. They haven't confirmed it had life. As far as we know, where there is water, there is life.

Why are we as a species ready to go to war at any time, whether it's for protest, for land, for a God, for a religion, or for man-made borders that separate us? You can literally be dying of starvation or be killed by your own government. Drug cartels and gangs or freedom fighters may be a few feet away, but because a border says you are not from this side, people can't help—unless you have oil or resources they can use. Humans will kill millions if they have to, in order to teach that their god is more peaceful and has more love than other gods. It's amazing how, when you study history, you see that thousands of wars were in the name of God or gods. We fight for freedom, which we should all have. Is this in our DNA from the Anunnaki, inherited from our creators? Are we meant to be warriors, to be ready for war at any time? Or are we simply a violent test tube species gone wrong? Though we're violent and unpredictable, one thing is for sure: we are survivors.

After the Great Flood, Enlil changed his mind about putting man into extinction. They gave us temples, and very few were chosen to be kings; some were even half Anunnaki, half human (a god-king). The Nibirians and Anunnaki themselves no longer had to physically work on earth. They probably disguised themselves as fish-humans, eagle-humans, lion-humans, and many other creatures to get the people to worship them as "gods" with the superior technology they have. It would make sense, or maybe they did have the power to physically change appearance to whatever they wish. In order to put fear on the people of not having an afterlife, they wanted man to worship them as gods.

In all ancient cultures, it is said that the people from the heavens, the star people, gave us language as a gift from the gods. Is this another coincidence?

Later on in history, the Pleiadians attempted to end the worship of the Nibirian (Anunnaki) gods in the land with the one-god concept. It did not last very long.

Let me tell you something about one famous Egyptian king, Akhenaten. He was the father of one of the most famous boy kings of all, Tutankhamun (King Tut). He was married to probably the second most famous Egyptian queen, Queen Nefertiti. He was a pharaoh of the eighteenth dynasty, and he ruled for seventeen years. During his reign, he abandoned traditional Egyptian polytheism (the worship of many gods) and introduced the worship of one true God, Aten. He is considered to be the first to claim there's one God. In his early days, his name was Amenhotep. He is believed to be the first half alien, half human king—a god-king!

According to Egyptian mythology, Akhenaten descended from the gods who arrived on earth at the time of Tep Zepi. Some still believe to this day that he did come from the stars. He was definitely the first and only to depict himself as short and chubby, with womanlike breasts, a potbelly, an elongated skull, and a very odd body. He did not look like any other pharaoh in history. All others had the perfect shoulders, flat stomachs, and a strong and masculine look. Akhenaten looked weak. Why would he do this? Could he have been half alien and half human—an alien hybrid? Could he have been Anunnaki? Could have he carried the blood of Anunnaki? He claimed, "There is one God, my father. I can approach him by day and by night." Who is he, and how can he approach his creator?

Many elongated skulls have been found around the globe with very little explanation or very silly theories. When they don't know how to explain it, we always get, "We need more tests. We need to dig deeper."

Let's get into elongated skulls. They are not found only in Egypt but also many other countries, such as ancient Mesoamerica (from Mexico to Central America, to South America), Africa, and even Russia. One of the most famous was discovered in 1928 by Julio Tello. I have seen TV shows and read many articles about this. One article I found was from www.ferocesmente.com, and the article came out on June 14, 2016. Let me share with you what was found.

In 1928, Peruvian archaeologist Julio Tello made one of the most mysterious discoveries during his excavations. Tello discovered a complex and sophisticated graveyard under a harsh soil of the Paracas Desert. Tello discovered a set of controversial human remains. This discovery has baffled scientists for a long time, and some scientists don't want to research or study these skulls; they're scared to be ridiculed by their peers or lose their jobs in case something magnificent is discovered—or better yet, in case these skulls were to tell us they were not human at all. The bodies in the tombs had some of the largest elongated skulls ever discovered on the planet, now known as the Paracas skulls.

The Peruvian archaeologist discovered over three hundred skulls, which are believed to be over three thousand years old. The cranium of the skulls are at least 25 percent larger and up to 60 percent heavier than the skulls of regular human beings. Researchers firmly believe that these traits could not have been achieved through head bindings, as some researchers suggest. Not only are they different in weight, but the Paracas skulls are also structurally different and only have one parietal plate, whereas ordinary humans have two. Here, we have a situation that some of these skulls were found with red hair. This is not common for people in that part of the world. The fact is they don't know who they were or where they came from. Were these skulls ancient Anunnaki gods?

One amazing skull discovered later was that of a baby no more than three to five months. Not only did it have an elongated skull, but it had a reddish color of hair, which of course is not typical of the natives that live in the region part of the world. The skull dates back as far as 2,800 years ago. The baby was too young to have a head binding ritual from the parents. It was not old enough to have developed an elongated skull unless he or she was already born with it. Could these skulls be Anunnaki or some other type of alien being? Or is it another coincidence that three hundred unknown, humanlike beings were buried in the exact same area? These skulls worldwide are connected to kings, ancient soldiers, pharaohs, queens, the elite, and god-kings all around the globe. We see depictions in Egypt, Central America, Mesopotamia, South America, and many other parts of the world with beings with these skulls.

We must keep our eyes to the stars. We should study, read, and educate ourselves. We should read books that matter, learning one theory and then another with a totally different view. We should read about different myths and religions, as well as the different gods of Greece, Rome, Egypt, Central America, and so on. We should learn the stories and myths of Native Americans. There are worlds that you cannot imagine. You can make up your own belief of our true origin, but that is one story out of hundreds that are out there. Open your mind to the impossible. Think and read outside the box; a new world awaits you. Who knows? Maybe you will be our next great archaeologist or scientist who will make a change. It all starts with a book.

This is my interpretation of the research and many books and articles that I have read of the Anunnaki, the life, and planets that are out there in our universe.

NIBIRU

(Planet X)

Now let's get into some Nibiru facts that might be true. First, let me explain that NASA calls it Planet X. They have seen it, and they have noticed it there is something out there. The believers call it Nibiru.

Several ancient texts from Mesopotamia have strong evidence that supports theories that Nibiru has an orbital period of 3,600 years. The number 3,600 was represented by the Sumerians as a large circle, a shar.

Nibiru is believed to be four to five times bigger than the earth—a gigantic rocky planet. It is a magnetic planet, and it is suggested that it would cause the earth to tilt in space as it passes. It is also believed that it would cause days of obscurity while passing next to other planets, possibly even stopping their rotation during its transition across space due to its powerful magnetic properties.

Some researchers believe if a planet like Nibiru comes close to earth, it would cause chaos, volcanic eruptions, earthquakes, and tsunamis, creating an entirely new geography and climate. Nibiru in the Kolbrin, a parallel Bible located in the Monastery of Glastonbury, Scotland, is known as the Destroyer.

Only the wise know where it went and that it shall return at the appointed time. It is the Destroyer, and it's color was bright and fierce and ever-changing with an unstable appearance—a fierce body of flames.

In 2008, Japanese researchers announced that according to their calculations, there should be an undiscovered planet. It could be the size of two to three times the size of earth. If their calculations are correct, this would support Sitchin's theory of the existence of Nibiru.

Let's go back a little further in time, to December 30, 1983. The *Washington Post* had a very interesting article written by Thomas O'Toole. Let's take a look.

> A heavenly body possibly as large as the giant planet Jupiter and possibly so close to Earth that it would be part of this solar system has been found in the direction of the constellation Orion by an orbiting telescope aboard the U.S infrared astronomical satellite.

> The most fascinating explanation of this mystery body, is that it is a giant gaseous planet as large as Jupiter and close to Earth as close as 50 trillion miles. While that may seem like a great distance in Earth bound terms, it is a stone's throw in cosmological terms, so close in fact that it would be the nearest heavenly body to Earth beyond the outermost planet Pluto.

> The mysterious planet was seen twice by the infrared satellite as it scanned the sky. A second observation took place six months after the first and suggested the mystery planet had not moved from its spot in the sky near the western edge of the constellation Orion at that time.

> When IRAS scientists first saw this planet it was then calculated that it could be as close as 50 trillion miles, there was some speculation that it might be moving towards Earth.

On July 13, 1987, there was a *Newsweek* article that said NASA disclosed there might be a tenth planet orbiting our sun. According to NASA research scientist John Anderson, "Planet X might actually be out there, but nowhere near our planets."

Very interesting, right? Many other articles came out months and years after this, following the discovery. Now, mind you, this was 1983; new studies have been made, and we have better technology. It was not until later that NASA started calling it Planet X.

The scientific community dismissed the idea of another planet in our solar system with a strange orbit. Zecharia Sitchin knew about it, and he wrote about it in his 1976 book *The 12ᵗʰ Planet*. Now the question we must ask is, What else did he get right?

Let's go to January 8, 2017. The show is called *60 Minutes* on CBS. The segment "The Hunt for Planet Nine," with Bill Whitaker reporting. What follows is some of the transcript from this interview.

His interview was with astronomer at Caltech, Mike Brown, he is credited with being the astronomer "who killed Pluto," Pluto, had been considered a planet for 76 years. But Pluto lost its planet status after astronomer Brown discovered that Pluto wasn't so special. Brown and other astronomers have since found hundreds of large balls of ice like Pluto, circling the sun, at the far reaches of our solar system. Demoting Pluto leaves us with eight planets. But Mike Brown is sure there is a real ninth planet way out far beyond Pluto. He believes the real Planet Nine is huge and it's out there. Brown and his team of scientists think that it's somewhere between 10 and 20 times more massive than Earth. He also believes this new planet is about 50 billion miles away, that is not very far, and he suggests that it has a 15,000 year orbit! 15,000 years to go around our sun. Could this be Nibiru? Could have Sitchin missed the orbit of Nibiru by a mere 11,000 year.

Konstantin Batygin, Brown's partner a planetary science professor at Caltech, came up with mathematical proof. That Planet Nine is pulling those remote objects in similar oblong orbits. Batygin equations melds 10 accepted formulas, and when coupled with more than 8,000 lines of computer code it describes Planet Nine's orbit. He also doesn't have to see it to know it exists. All mathematical calculations that planet nine exists.

First Brown is certain that Planet Nine is there, and he thinks that by looking at the pictures, it can take up to fifteen thousand years to orbit the sun. He never explained from where that conclusion came. It seemed like he was trying to tell us there was a Planet Nine in our solar system. They never mentioned Planet X. Why? If Planet X is in the Orion Constellation, and this new planet is beyond that, are we talking about two new possibilities? And you would think Whitaker would at least ask, "Do you believe it might have life? Is that our tenth planet? Could this be Nibiru?"

Sometimes confusion seems to be the name of the game. They'll tell us one thing, let time pass, and then tell us something totally different. I understand there is no certainty in science, but just once I'd like to get facts. Even if it hurts, and even if it will change every belief I have, I would rather have the facts as they are. But I guess truth can be stranger than fiction. I for one would rather have the truth.

On February 22, 2017, NASA announced that they found not one, but seven earthlike exoplanets! Three of the seven are said to be in the habitable zone, also known as the Goldilocks zone. The earthlike planets orbit a star called TRAPPIST-1 in the Aquarius constellation. It is a mere 39 light-years away, approximately 235 trillion miles—a trip around the block in universe talk. The Milky Way is said to be 100,000 light-years wide, so 39 light-years is basically our next-door cosmic neighbor.

TRAPPIST stands for Transiting Planets and Planetesimals Small Telescopes.

7 Earth-Size Planets Orbit Dwarf Star, NASA and European Astronomers say.

Not just one, but seven Earth-size planets that could potentially harbor life have been identified orbiting a tiny star not far away, offering the first realistic opportunity to search for signs of alien life outside our solar system.

The orientation of the orbits of the seven planets allows them to be studied with great detail they said.

Several of the planets can contain ocean waters, and are rocky worlds, astronomers said, based on the distance of the planets from their sun. The Journal Nature published the findings Wednesday 22nd of February 2017.

Scientists could even discover evidence of aliens. Are we finally getting close to a real answer from the governments?

All seven Planets are very close to their sun, circling more quickly than the planets in our solar system. The innermost completes an orbit in just 1.5 days. The farthest planet completes an orbit in about 20 days.

Because the planets are so close to a cool reddish sun, their surfaces could be at the right temperatures to have water flow, considered one of the essential ingredients for life.

The fourth, fifth, and sixth planets orbit in the star's "habitable zone," where the planets could sport oceans. So far that is just speculation, they have confirmed for the two innermost planets that they are not enveloped in hydrogen. That means they are rocky like Earth.

Because the planets are so close to TRAPPIST-1, they have quite likely become "gravitationally locked" to the star, always with one side of the planets facing the star, much as it is always the same side of Earth's moon facing Earth. That would mean one side would be warmer, but an atmosphere would distribute heat, and the scientists said that would not be an insurmountable obstacle for life.

"The Discovery gives us a hint that finding a second earth is not a matter of if, but when," Thomas Zurbuchen said.

I think with this conference, it was a step forward for NASA and the governments around the world to let us know there is life out there! However, maybe that we have been visited by extraterrestrials for thousands of years. Slowly they are giving us information, bit by bit. I believe there will be full alien disclosure within the next five years. You can only keep secrets for so long before something happens and the truth comes out. I wish people would educate themselves about the possibilities of life on other planets and not fear what they don't know. To question their religion and their God just because there is life in another galaxy, another solar system is silly. If God so loves us and created us, why would he not create more life elsewhere? Or are all the solar systems, the billions of planets, the trillions of stars a big waste of space? I refuse to believe that.

Astronomers announced in early 2017 that data from Hawaii's Keck Observatory had evidence of perhaps as many as 114 new exoplanets. They made observations of over 1,600 stars for a period of twenty years. One planet discovered, Gliese 411b, is getting a lot of attention from astronomers because it's a rocky super-earth planet. We also have a planet named Proxima B, which is about four light-years away—only about six trillion miles. It's a matter of time. Keep your eyes to the sky ...

Now, let's get back to Nibiru. Nibiru arrives in our solar system every 3,600 hundred years, moving clockwise. That means when coming toward earth, we would cross paths like oncoming traffic and a head-collision. This is how the Anunnaki would travel from Nibiru to earth without light-years of travel. Earth would not collide with Nibiru, but it would be close enough to cause some damage such as volcanic eruptions, earthquakes, and tsunamis. There'd be massive chaos with humans, and it would seem like the end of life as we know it.

It is also written in ancient Sumerian texts that it originates from the Orion Constellation. Once it does orbit around the sun after passing earth, it will continue on its path in space and disappear into the stars for another 3,600 years. It would not collide with earth, because if it was going to do that, it would have happened a very long time ago, both earth and Nibiru would not be here. Some theorize that the last time it came was about thirteen thousand years ago, causing the Great Flood, but that's one theory out of many.

Mythologically speaking, based on what the ancient texts found and translated tell us, Nibiru is real and not a myth.

Also, we should ask whether Nibiru had anything to do with the extinction of dinosaurs. It is said that earth has gone through three massive extinction periods: the Ice Age, the Great Flood, and a massive asteroid (which allegedly killed the dinosaurs). Might have Nibiru and the Anunnaki been involved? There are theories that the Anunnaki wiped out the dinosaurs with their massive weapons of destruction to inhabit the earth. It is estimated that Nibiru will make its next appearance in the year 2900. What should we expect? Will they come back and judge us? Will they come back and be satisfied with what their creation has done to earth? Or will they be dissatisfied by the way we kill each other and treat the earth, and will they exterminate us and start all over again?

We must also ask ourselves if earth carries well over eight million species alone, how many life-forms would a planet the size of Nibiru carry? And how many other life forms from other planets would the Anunnaki have encountered? Could there be a real Star Wars galaxy out there? By that, I mean could they be traveling from one living planet to another? Are we really ants among the gods?

In almost every single ancient culture, we find an Anunnaki connection. Look around our ancient civilizations and the proof they left behind. Notice their ability to build massive monuments, to transport stones weighing hundreds of tons and put them together with precise engineering skills. Pyramids are almost identical from one side of the world to the other, thousands of miles apart in some cases.

It is believed that the Great Pyramids of Giza might be one hundred thousand years old, but at the same time, others believe that they were built after the Great Flood, and that many more, older pyramids lay under the sands, the waters, and the jungles all around the globe. Some countries such as China and a few others hide theirs with trees and grass to make them look natural. Why? Yet we are told that the ancients had no means to travel that far, or the technology and ability to cross oceans. But country after country, across deserts and deep oceans, we see pyramids almost identical to each other.

Many civilizations have the same stories. The Gods came from the heavens and gave us life and language. Many kings and pharaohs in ancient

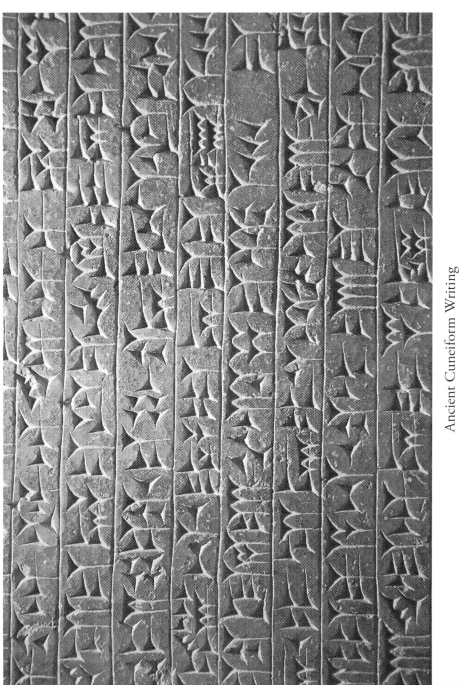

Ancient Cuneiform Writing

times around the globe were worshipped as gods because many people believed they were godlike—meaning they were either half alien or half star people, and they were worshipped as such. Could it be possible that the Anunnaki or other alien life forms helped us? Did they put certain half-breeds (half alien, half human) in power for their own agenda, their own purposes? Did they give them kingships? Many Anunnaki were considered gods, and one of many reasons was because their life span is superior to ours. We are lucky to make it to 100 years old, but because of the way Nibiru travels around the solar system, one year for the Anunnaki is 3,600 for us. Just imagine: ten years for the Anunnaki is 36,000 years for us! They lived for centuries in our world. Of course they would be considered gods! Think of the knowledge, the science, and the wisdom one could gain with such a life span.

Our planet is believed to be 4.5 billion years old. Imagine a world much older than ours—let's say 20 billion years old—with intelligent life for 10 billion years. Can you imagine what kind of technology they would be capable of having? We barely made it to the moon in 1969, not even fifty years ago. Now look how far we have come. We have robots on Mars! Imagine what technology we will have five billion years from now. We could have summer homes on Saturn. Okay, now I'm dreaming—but why not? With the right technology, anything is possible. So why is it impossible to think there might be another world far more advanced than ours?

This brings us to the Weld-Blundell prism, better known as the Sumerian Kings list. The Sumerians are considered to have the very first civilization, the first written language, advanced technology such as astronomy, mathematics, pottery, jewelry, and so on.

The cuneiforms containing the Kings List lists kings going back over 100,000 years, as well as the history of kings ruling over 230,000 years. One god-king named Alaljar ruled for 36,000 years. Some theorize that with eight kings alone, they ruled 241,000 years. How is this even possible? Their life span is likely far greater than ours. The Antideluvian (before the flood) kings list does describe godly or hybrid kings that would rule 10,000–20,000 years or more. There are famous biblical kings, and there are what some try to tell us are "mythical" kings. The question would be,

Tile with Sumerian writing.

why would they go through all this trouble to write down their kings, battles, kingships, and mythical kings? It makes no sense. The mythical kings are said to rule for thousands of years. Then we have Gilgamesh, who is also on this list. He is said to have ruled over 120 years. He was considered to be half god, half human—maybe half alien, half human. He did consider himself a god-king.

The Bible plainly teaches early patriarchs often lived to be about one thousand years old, with some having children when they were several hundred years old. Enoch (Gen. 5:23) survived the Great Flood and is said to have lived over nine hundred years. Noah lived over 950 years (Gen. 5:31). This is written in the Bible, so why is the Kings List so hard to believe? Why does it sound so impossible? Is it easier to believe because it is in the Bible and not in cuneiform? The Bible speaks of the Great Flood; the Sumerian Kings List speaks of the flood. Many ancient cultures speak of long life spans: Greeks, Romans, Chinese, Babylonians, and many others. The same goes for the Great Flood. How is this a coincidence?

The Weld-Blundell prism cuneiform objects are at the Ashmolean Museum at the University of Oxford.

After the Great Flood, we don't hear much about anyone living long lives. Why? It seems like maybe they were godly, and maybe most if not all died with the Great Flood; the survivors lived their remaining days on Earth in secret. Could they be the Watchers, the Fallen of Earth from the heavens? Could they have been half Anunnaki? Were they the Gods who took daughters of man and made them wives, where the children who were born were considered godly?

Enlil hated the fact that Nibirians were taking earth wives. He was not happy with the chaos and the rapid population boom by the humans. When Enlil found out the flood was coming, he told the Anunnaki, Enki, and Ninmah to be ready to go to the heavens and to not warn the humans that a great flood was coming. Sitchin teaches us that the Anunnaki knew the Great Flood was coming—not as punishment for our sins but because it was the last of the ice age. The earth was tilting, and the huge icebergs in the north and south were breaking apart, causing massive waves that covered the earth.

Enki went behind Enil's back and told Utnapishtim (biblical Noah) to build a vessel (ark) and fill it up with men, women, children, animals, and other living creatures.

Enlil and the Anunnaki got in their spaceships and watched the Great Flood, safe in the skies. They watched the destruction and death from the heavens. Yes, the "gods" got on their spaceships and left us for extermination. Enlil was furious when he found out what Enki had done.

It seems that the father of humanity as we know it would be Enki. Enki sought to free the humans from the enslavement of the Anunnaki by having Tiamat/Eve eat from the Tree of Knowledge, which essentially was some kind of an awaking of consciousness. The fruit from the Tree of Knowledge made Tiamat/Eve and Adamu become fully conscious and self-aware. It was Enki who told Utnapishtim/Noah about the great storm, advising him to build a vessel big enough to carry animals and some humans. He taught Utnapishtim/Noah how to build it. It was Enki who saved man from extinction.

Enlil saw the survivors, and somehow he was impressed and had a feast with them.

Shortly after the flood, the Anunnaki had to build new temples, new pyramids. There was a new geography on earth. This is when they gave kingships to not just god-kings but also human kings. They picked the chosen few who would rule the earth on their behalf.

Robert Ballard is an underwater archaeologist best known for his 1985 discovery of the *Titanic*. Ballard believes that much of the earth was covered in ice. "Where I live in Connecticut was ice a mile above my house, all the way back to the North Pole, about 15 million kilometers, that's a big ice cube," he said in an *ABC News* interview.

According to Ballard, when the glaciers started melting, it rushed through the earth's rivers, lands, and oceans, causing gigantic waves of destruction—a catastrophic flood around the world. Ballard says this happened about twelve to thirteen thousand years ago—exactly the time frame Zecharia Sitchin suggests.

Now, let's look at some beautiful pyramids. I will tell you a few facts about them, but notice how similar they are to each other. Remember the great temple of Ur in the beginning of the book, and then think, *How was this possible? Why are they all shaped so similarly? How were they made with such precise engineering skills? How can slaves transport precisely cut rocks weighing multiple tons? Some quarries were as far as five hundred miles away, so how was this possible?* For some pyramids, it was not the distance that was amazing. Some were so high in the mountaintops that even for us today, it would be impossible to carry such a large, heavy stone over rough terrain. And we are not talking about a few stones. In some cases, we are talking about millions of heavy stones, perfectly put together on top of another. We can't even put a piece of paper between two stones—this is how perfectly they were built.

Machu Picchu is a beautiful, amazing city. There are not enough words to describe this place. Peru itself is full of ancient mystery, from Machu Picchu to Cusco, to the Nazca lines, to the Paracas skulls. Peru needs a hundred books written about the mysteries that it holds. Machu Picchu is positioned on top of the Andes mountains, 7,970 feet above sea level. It's an ancient Incan city. We say Incan, but it is believed the city was already in ruins when the Incas inhabited the area. One can see the difference in the stone work on parts of the area, and height wise, that is nothing compared to Cusco, which is 11,152 feet above sea level.

Besides the obvious question about how the Incas could build these cities with the certainty of altitude sickness, what about carrying carry millions and millions of heavy stones? Why would they build them so high, to make it hard as humanly possible? Did they have help? Were they trying to reach the heavens and get closer to the gods? Or could it be that maybe these two cities above sea level now were built after the Great Flood and there was no land underneath it? What if it was all water and the Gods helped with the building? Zecharia Sitchin wrote Enlil was so impressed man survived the Great Flood that he decided to let man live. He changed his mind about the extinction of man, which he helped create. So why wouldn't the gods help or direct the right way to build Machu Picchu? It seems there was a lot of work to build this great city, and for what? Survival? Maybe it was a spaceport, where it was easier for the Anunnaki to land, control their slaves, and check on the progress of whatever mission was needed in Machu Picchu. It would be easier to land and fly away when needed. Many pyramids or temples were built with a flat top. Why? Were they landing ports?

Here are some personal pictures of Machu Picchu.

Today, we cannot come close to forming rocks like this without heating them to well over five thousand degrees. Even then, putting them together to take that shape is unlikely. Scientists can't give us a believable theory on who built this city and how. There is no record who built it; when the Incas discovered it, it was already in ruin. Who were the people who built this, and where did they go? Look at the perfectly cut stones. You can't put a piece of paper or razor between these stones. Yet mainstream scientists tell us this was made with ancient tools—no wheels to transport them, no technology.

Did they have otherworldly, intelligent help with far superior technology?

Viracocha was the almighty god of the Incas (also known as Wiro Qocha, Huiracocha, and Wiraqoca). He is the father of all gods, the creator of heaven and earth, the sun and moon, and all living things. Other gods were given the duties to watch over the human race until his return. Viracocha promised one day to return. As legend has it, even from afar, to this day he still watches the progress of his children.

Could Viracocha have been Anu, an Anunnaki god? He is believed to return one day, but from where? The heavens? Nibiru? Another celestial star?

Puma Punku in Bolivia is another beautiful ancient site full of mystery. There, you can also find stone blocks perfectly cut and weighing 85 metric tons. The biggest stones weigh well over 130 metric tons. Amazing! How is this possible? How was this ancient site erected? This site is most famous for being the H block site, meaning many of the stones are shaped like the capital letter *H* and look like they were cut with advanced, sophisticated technology. There is no other explanation.

Could have these sites been Anunnaki connected? Or could it have been a different type of extraterrestrial being?

Then there's Easter Island, a Polynesian island in the southeastern Pacific Ocean. There are about nine hundred gigantic stone figures that date back thousands of years. The tallest of these stones is about 75 feet and weighs over 170 tons. Most are about thirteen feet tall. These monolithic human figures are also known as the Moai Statues.

It's very interesting when you see pictures of these statues, like they are standing guard and protecting the land. Each one of them is said to watch

The Great Egyptian Sphinx of Giza

over a different part of the world. Some are believed to still be buried in the volcanic crater. Why were they built? What's their purpose? Were they simply made to scare off any enemies, but our imaginations get the better of us? Could it be that simple, or do they have a higher meaning—one we cannot understand yet?

Egypt is one of my favorite places to study! Ancient Egypt is full of beauty, mystery, and elegance. Everything about ancient Egypt fascinates me—the gods, the legends, the stories, and the myths.

Carved from the bedrock of the Giza Plateau, this mythical creature with the body of a lion and the head of a human is known as the Great Egyptian Sphinx, or the Sphinx of Egypt. I prefer the Great Egyptian Sphinx because it sounds cool.

This monument stands on the west bank of the Nile River in Giza, Egypt. Scholars believe it was built by the ancient Egyptians during the kingship of the Pharaoh Khafre (son of Khufu, also known as Cheops) during 2558–2532 BC. It is almost 240 feet long; the paws alone are about 62 feet high. This gigantic limestone figure is definitely one of the world's oldest and most famous monuments. There are also theories that it did not always have the head of a man, but maybe Anubis, the great god of the afterlife and the underworld. Or a lion head, the head of a canine or a head of a jackal.

To this day, we cannot get an exact explanation on who built it and when. There was nothing written or inscribed on this great monument about who built it and why. Scientists, Egyptologists, geologists, and archaeologists continue to debate its history. Some say it was made 4,500 years ago, and some theories have Khufu building it. I have read theories that suggest it was constructed up to fifteen thousand years ago. The most amazing and interesting theory came in October 2008: the Great Egyptian Sphinx is 800,000 years old! At the International Conference of Geoarchaeology and Archaeomineralogy, held in Sofia, Ukraine, scientists Manichev Vjacheslav I (Institute of Environmental Geochemistry of the National Academy of Sciences of Ukraine) and Alexander G. Parkhomenenko (Institute of Geography of the National Academy of sciences of Ukraine) presented a paper with this claim. "Geological Aspect of the Problem of Dating the Great Egyptian Sphinx Construction" is the title of their work. In a few simple pages, they conclude that the Great Sphinx has many signs of erosion, and that it was probably underwater for a very long period of time.

I will give you their conclusion; I suggest if you are interested in reading the rest, you can research it yourself. That's what's great about today's technology: your phone can take you back many lifetimes ago by pressing a few letters. All you do is write down the title in Google, and boom!

Their conclusion?

> A comparison of the formation of wave-cut hollows on the sea coasts with erosion structures in the form of hollows observed on the surface of the Great Egyptian Sphinx permits a conclusion about the similarity of the formation mechanism. It is connected to water activity in large water bodies during the Sphinx submersion for a long period of time. Geological data from literary sources can suggest a possible Sphinx submersion in the Early Pleistocene, and its initial construction is believed to date from the time of most ancient history.

Now we are left with more questions than ever before! The mystery keeps getting better. Who built it, and why? The Great Sphinx—protector of Egypt!

Our time here is like a star in the universe, the moon, and the galaxies. The truth is out there. If you seek to find the truth about our alien origin or our human origin, you must take everything written in old books, texts, cuneiforms, tablets, and the Bible and read them from a scientific point of view. We are the future. We must read and realize that thousands of years ago, the ancients interpreted things in a much different way. See it through their eyes. It is up to you to teach yourself this reality, or else you will never understand.

The Great Temple of Ramses II is also known as the Nubian Monuments and the Temple of Abu Simbel. It is located in southern Nubia. It is said that it got the name Abu Simbel after a young local boy helped the explorers find it. Ramses's reign (ca. 1279–1213 BCE) is maybe the longest reign of Egypt's imperial age. The temple incorporates accounts of the events of his reign. It is located near the border of Sudan, on the western banks of Lake Nasser. How amazing is this monument? The size alone is mind-boggling! Can you imagine what it looked like in its prime?

The Great Pyramids of Giza

Yet we are told a stick and sharp rocks can build temples such as this. I like to show pictures with people in them so my friends can see the magnitude of these ancient temples.

The largest pyramid in Giza is in the center: the Great Pyramid of Giza. It's believed that Khufu had it built around 2560 BC, and it's estimated that there are over 2.3 million stone rocks, each weighing about 2.5 tons. Some stones weigh as much as 50 tons! Scholars believe it took about 20 years to build it. Impossible! There are 2,300,000 blocks, perfectly cut and placed one on top of another. That means they would have to stack one after another within two minutes each, perfectly aligned with no mistakes twenty-four hours a day for twenty-three years. The truth is they don't know, and the ancient Egyptians didn't know who built it either. The ancient Egyptians never have taken credit for building the Great Pyramid, the Great Sphinx, or the Osirion. They never claimed to be the first people to inhabit Egypt.

Even Egyptian myths say that the ancient Egyptians enjoyed exceptionally advanced technologies and mystical systems, which were actually the legacy of that older culture that somehow ended by some kind of catastrophe. It is believed by ancient alien theorists that the Great Pyramid and the Sphinx were already there, abandoned when the first Egyptians habited the area. If this is the oldest of the pyramids, why are the rest that followed not as perfect and not as high? Why aren't they as perfectly engineered? You do not go backward with technology. Anything that followed the Great Pyramid should have been greater in all aspects. It makes no sense. However, it does make sense if it was there before the ancient Egyptians made it their home. So who built it? Could this be the living proof that ancient alien technology built it?

Some believe it was some sort of power plant, a beacon, or some kind of energy source that would receive and deliver energies to the heavens, maybe to a mother ship. To this day, we cannot duplicate this enormous ancient pyramid, not with all the technology we possess. Yet somehow it was made over ten thousand years ago with rope and ancient tools? The ancients somehow managed to build it and other magnificent temples, cities, pyramids around the globe. Here too we have gods that ruled for thousands of years—god-kings! Were they Anunnaki, or Anunnaki hybrids? No matter where we look, there is an Anunnaki connection.

Teotihuacan Pyramids, Mexico

The Osirion is just as mysterious as the Great Sphinx and the Great Pyramid. It also has stone blocks as heavy as one hundred tons. We don't know who built it, or when. The quarry is said to be in Aswan, which is a little over three hundred miles away! How is that possible? Seti I's temple was built over it, and some Egyptologists suggest it is part of the same building, but it was built at a very much lower level than the foundations of the Temple of Seti. Seti ruled from 1294–1279 BC. This is another mystery, and no one agrees on anything about the construction, the time period, and who built it.

The Anunnaki connection is there because the myths, legends, stories, or actual facts (depending how you interpret it) match, even with the Bible. Horus, the god-king of Egypt, was born of a virgin, walked on water, was resurrected, had twelve disciples, performed miracles, and raised someone from the dead. The difference is his tale was written about 3,500 years before Jesus was said to walk the earth. Very interesting, isn't it? Could it have been translated wrong? Or could the Jesus story have been borrowed from Egyptian mythology? Was it mythology at all? Could it have been true, and only the names are different? Why are the stories so similar? There have been plenty of books written about the similarities, but that's a different subject. My point is that one person's mythology is another person's interpretation of the truth. So what are we to believe?

Could Horus have been Anunnaki, a true god? Horus is always depicted as human with a falcon head, or just a falcon. In some depictions, he's the falcon with a crown on its head. How could he transform himself from human to falcon? Or was he half human, half falcon? Did he have superior technology to transform himself so that the people would worship him—not magic, but technology? We see magicians today making cars and people disappear, but it's a trick of the eye. Why wouldn't an intelligent being with superior technology not know how to trick the masses?

In the picture of the Teotihuacan Pyramids, you can clearly see people exploring the pyramids, so you can see how massive they are. This is what I mean about the step pyramids with flat tops. It looks like a helicopter can land with no problem, right? It's like a spaceship port, where ships can land and take off at will.

Teotihuacan Pyramids, Mexico (Pyramid of the Moon)

This magnificent site is known as the birthplace of the gods. The Aztecs believed that the gods created the universe at this site. Again we hear a similar story. When the Aztecs arrived at Teotihuacan, the city was already in ruins, abandoned. This was around 300 BC. We have beautiful pyramids around Mexico, Honduras, Guatemala, Belize, El Salvador, and all throughout Central America. It is believed that the Great Mayan civilization held a population of over twenty million people; Teotihuacan alone inhabited 120,000–200,000 people. Where did they go? The Americas have more pyramid structures than the rest of the globe combined because the Mayans, Olmecs, Aztecs, and Incas ruled there.

Quetzalcoatl was the supreme, almighty god of ancient Meso-America. He was called the Plumed Serpent and was depicted as a mix of a bird and a snake. He was the creator of earth and humankind, and he was the god of wind and rain. He invented the calendar and is also considered the god of agriculture, science, the arts, and learning. (Sound familiar? Could this have been Enki?) Many buildings and temples were dedicated to this god.

According to the Mayan calendar, on December 2012 humankind entered a new era: the return of Quetzalcoatl and the galactic rebirth of the sun, Hunab Ku. Hunab Ku is the invisible god of gods, the supreme god and ultimate creator.

Quetzalcoatl was a flesh-and-blood god that walked the earth. The Mayan civilization was definitely one like the Egyptians and Sumerians, with such precise studies in astronomy, math, architecture, and many other things. There was nothing primitive about the knowledge they had. The Mayans are also known for having a fully developed written language.

Quetzalcoatl said before he went to the heavens that he would return, and when he returned, he would see and judge his creation that he'd left on this planet. Where did he go? Was he Anunnaki? Did he get on a spaceship and head back to the heavens, to Nibiru? As legend has it, are we to wait for his return?

Is it possible that Quetzalcoatl and Viracocha are the same god? Their descriptions and characteristics from the inhabitants of Central and South America do not match what the ancient Incas or Mayans would look like, with grayish red beards, white skin, blue eyes. Were these ancient deities Anunnaki?

Chichen Itza Pyramid, Mexico

When researching the gods from the Aztecs, Olmecs, Mayans, and Incas, we find stories and myths of the gods who left earth, promising to return one day.

The depictions of Viracocha are very similar to the ancient gods of the Sumerians, with long beards and mustaches. For ancient Mesoamerican, South American Indians did not have facial hair such as beards and mustaches. Even North American Indians are not known to have facial hair.

Mayans, Aztecs, Incas, and Olmecs were brown or dark-skinned people with brown eyes, and they were not known to be very tall. Why are their gods depicted with white skin and blue eyes, and why are they much taller than the natives? If they were Anunnaki or other extraterrestrial beings, it's not farfetched to think these Gods would travel from one area to another to be worshipped as gods. That way, the Anunnaki could have the people do the work they desired. Could these gods be one, or is this another ancient coincidence? We sure seem to have a lot of those.

Also, if we pay attention to how similar these pyramids are around the globe, why are they made so similarly? What's the purpose? Are they all connected somehow? Are they still connected with some kind of technology we don't see or understand? Were they trying to reach the gods? Were they built by the gods? Or are they some kind of ancient alien technology that we don't yet understand?

Human sacrifice was definitely one of the rituals to satisfy the gods in Mesoamerica, or at least to try to get their attention. They made offerings of blood to please the gods. Were there any human beings around at the time the structures were being built? Were we even created yet? Did the Anunnaki build them before Enki and Ninmha biologically engineered their creations with the genetic manipulation they gave early Homo erectus, or do the pyramids date even farther back in time, hundreds of thousands of years before Adamu and Tiamat?

Sitchin suggests that the Anunnaki life spans were 120 sars (a sar is what the Anunnaki called an orbit around the sun, 3,600 of our years) which is 432,000 years according to the King List. This is a long time to live, so why couldn't have they built the pyramids themselves? This would explain why early ancients would consider them gods: they outlive you, your grandparents, your great-grandparents, and so on. Why wouldn't

The Astronaut

and the Spider of Nazca, Peru

they consider them gods? If the Anunnaki were the first to inhabit ancient Mesopotamia, they still needed bases around the globe to search for the resources they needed. Why wouldn't they build these great structures? Maybe the pyramids were some kind of energy source that helped them travel back and forth faster, or they're some kind of satellites that helped them communicate with the leaders of Nibiru or the mothership in the heavens, waiting for them to load whatever gold and other resources. Or could they be some kind of intergalactic portal that took the Anunnaki from one planet to another?

Time and time again, no matter where you look, there lies more mystery after mystery. If there were approximately twenty million Mayans throughout Central America—where did they go? The same goes for the pre-Incas, the first Egyptians, and the people of Easter island. How did all these civilizations disappear? Was there a catastrophe? Were they gone before the Great Flood, or did they perish with it? Were they taken away to the heavens to keep doing the gods' work? Were they lined up like sheep and taken to Nibiru, to be slaves? Somehow we lost our history, our true origins. Somehow we woke up one day and had a worldwide case of amnesia! Were we somehow programmed to forget? In order to start all over, did they drop the seed of man and woman, leaving the few they didn't take to start all over again?

The Astronaut and the Spider are some of many figures you can see in Nazca, known as the Nazca lines in South of Peru. You can see different animals and plants. There are about 300 of these lines, and some of the largest figures are 1,200 feet. You also have lines that run for miles and miles. The whole area is a mystery. Who made them, and why? The most amazing thing about this area is that you can only see them from the sky; you have to be very high on a mountaintop, or in a helicopter or small airplane, to see what is on the ground.

Why would they go through all this trouble to make these figures and lines when one can only see them from the sky? Who were they signaling? Was this their way to communicate to the Gods? Or was it a way to say, "Come here. We're here"?'

In this same mysterious area, we have huge mountains. That doesn't sound incredible at all, I know, but one thing is missing: they have no tops. The tops of the mountains are completely cut off, flat almost to perfection. They look like an airport runway. Also, there is no dirt, rocks, or debris—nothing at the bottom of the mountains. So where did the top part disappear to? As if by magic, the top just disappears with no trace that it was ever there. Someone or something cut them off, or pressed down with something so massive that it flattened the tops.

What if it was some kind of extraterrestrial airport? Ancient astronaut theorists believe these were some type of ancient runways. It would make sense because Peru is one country where you can find almost all the resources and minerals one would look for when exploring a new world. Were the animals, plants, and figures to tell the gods, "You can find this here?" Was the Astronaut figure a way of telling the gods, "You've been here before. We welcome you?" One thing is for sure: no matter where you look, another ancient mystery remains, and everything always points to the heavens.

Now, let me take you to one of the most fascinating discoveries ever. When reading this, I was fascinated by possibilities something like this can bring to our search for our true origins, our real history—the history of man.

The following is by Dan Eden for Viewzone and Alexander Light for Humansarefree.com. The article is "Ancient Human Metropolis Found In Africa." I couldn't stop reading this news when I first read it, this amazing discovery can definitely change everything we know about our human origins. Something amazing is happening in South Africa as you read this. They discovered the remains of a huge metropolis that measures, about 1,500 square miles. It's part of an even larger community that is about 10,000 square miles, and they believe it to have been constructed about 160,000–200,000 BCE!

> The area is significant for one thing—gold. "The thousands of ancient gold mines discovered over the past 500 years, points to a vanished civilization that lived and dug for gold in this part of the world for thousands of years," says Tellinger. And if this is in fact the cradle of humankind, we may be looking at the activities of the oldest civilization on Earth.[2]

---

[2] http://www.viewzone2.com/adamscalendar22.html

In this article, he even gives coordinates to look for yourself. I suggest that you use Google Earth and start with the following coordinates.

Carolina—25.55' 53.28" S / 30.16' 13.13" E
Badplass – 25.47' 33.45" S / 30.40' 38.76" E
Waterval—25.38' 07.82" S / 30.21' 18.79" E
Machadodorp—25.39' 22.42" S / 30.17' 03.25"

These circular ruins are spread over a huge area. They can only be seen from the air or through modern satellite images. Some of the ruins have survived well enough to reveal their great size, with some circular walls very similar to those found in the Incan settlements in Peru. How could this be made by ancient humans when supposedly we were barely learning how to walk upright 200,000 years ago? How come the media is not all over this?

Here we have another great discovery but with no media, no headline news. Why? One would think such a great discovery would be all over the media. Or would it cause chaos because it might make you rethink everything you've been taught to believe? We will never evolve if we read one book, one thought; that means we will all think the same. One thing is for sure: if history teaches us anything, it is that knowledge, and wanting to learn and know more than what is taught, is a huge threat to authority.

Is it a coincidence that the three great pyramids of Egypt and the three great pyramids of Teotihuacan align to the Orion constellation? Zecharia Sitchin's theory is that Nibiru's orbit does come from the Orion constellation: Mintaka, Alnilam, Alnitak. Is this the most amazing coincidence? What are the odds? But wait—there is more. Even here in South Africa, we find Orion somehow involved. There is a bit more on the discovery in South Africa.

The first calculation of the age of the calendar were made based on the rise of Orion, a constellation known for its three stars forming the "Belt" of the mythical hunter.

The Earth wobbles on its axis and so the stars and constellations change their angle of presentation in the night sky on a cyclical basis. This rotation, called the "Precession" completes a cycle about every 26,000 years. By determining when the three stars of Orion's belt were positioned flat (horizontal) against the horizon, we can estimate the time when the three stones in the calendar were in alignment with these conspicuous stars.

The first rough calculation was at least 25,000 years ago. But new and more precise measurements kept increasing the age. The next calculation was presented by a master archaeoastronomer who wishes to remain anonymous for fear of ridicule by the ancient fraternity. His calculation was also based on the rise of Orion and suggested an age of at least 75,000 years. The most recent and most accurate calculation, done in June 2009, suggests an age of at least 160,000 years, based on the rise of Orion—flat on the horizon—but also the erosion of dolerite stones found at the site.

If this is something you would like to know more about, I strongly suggest Michael Tellinger's books: *Slave Species of the Gods, African Temples of the Anunnaki*, and *Adam's Calendar*, to start with. He also has a website that invites you to read about any new discoveries: www.michaeltellinger.com.

Orion is pretty popular with the ancients, from the Greeks to the Egyptians, South Africa, Mexico, Central America, and South America. Coincidence? Or did someone teach them—someone familiar with the heavens? South Africa is just like Peru and the Nazca lines; some go for miles and are very similar to each other. Why? What's the purpose? Maybe in ancient times, we did not worship or see God or gods, but they walked among us? The ancient Egyptians didn't think Osiris was myth, or Horus, and there are so many other gods in many other cultures around the globe. To the ancient people, these gods were flesh and blood like you and me.

One thing I don't understand is why mainstream scholars are so quick to say this is myth, this is a story, this is biblical, this is true. Even the city of Nineveh was considered a myth until it was discovered, along with its treasures. I'm not just talking about gold and artifacts—I'm talking about texts, scriptures, history, and writings. For someone like me finding literature about anything that has to do with ancient history is far more valuable than gold. Hopefully there is a linguist who can translate it to the truth, explaining what the words actually say, not what they meant to say. I for one would like to know the truth. There is already far too much evidence to think we are alone. We are not. My sun is visible to someone's wandering eyes, looking at his or her own night sky millions of miles away. Think about that.

There is an Anunnaki connection everywhere, and if it's not Anunnaki, there is an otherworldly intelligence connection. One can only deny for so long before the truth presents itself, and then you will have no choice but to face the truth and everything that comes with it.

Zecharia Sitchin, in *The 12ᵗʰ Planet,* explains his Anunnaki translation in great detail on page 410. He gives us an approximate timeline of an ancient past, and this is what he says.

445,000 years ago: The Anunnaki (biblical Nefilim), led by Enki, arrive on Earth from the twelfth Planet (Nibiru). Eridu—Earth Station 1—is established in southern Mesopotamia.

430,000 years ago: The great ice sheets begin to recede. A hospitable climate in the Near East.

415,000 years ago: Enki moves inland, establishes Larsa.

400,000 years ago: The great interglacial period spreads globally. Enlil arrives on Earth, establishes Nippur as Mission Control Center. Enki establishes sea routes to southern Africa, organizes gold-mining operations.

360,000 years ago: The Anunnaki (biblical Nefilim) establish Bad-Tibira as their metallurgical center for smelting and refining. Sippar, the spaceport, and other cities of the Gods are built.

300,000 years ago: The Anunnaki mutiny. Man-the "Primitive-Worker"—is fashioned be Enki and Ninhursag (Ninmah).

250,000 years ago: "Early Homo sapiens" multiply, spread to other continents.

200,000 years ago: Life on Earth regresses during new glacial period.

100,000 years ago: Climate warms again. The sons of the gods take the daughters of Man as wives.

77,000 Years ago: Ubartutu/Lamech, a human of divine parentage, assumes the reign in Shuruppak under the patronage if Ninhursag (Ninmah).

75,000 years ago: The "accursation of Earth"—a new ice age-begins. Regressive types of Man roam Earth.

49,000 years ago: The reign of Ziusudra ("Noah"), a "faithful servant" of Enki begins.

38,000 years ago: The harsh climatic period of the "seven passings" begins to decimate Mankind. Europe's Neanderthal Man disappears; only Cro-Magnon Man (based in the Near East) survives. Enlil, disenchanted with Mankind, seeks its demise.

13,000 years ago: The Nefilim, aware of the impending tidal wave that will be triggered by the nearing Twelfth Planet (Nibiru), vow to let Mankind perish. The Deluge (Great Flood) sweeps over Earth, abruptly ending the ice age.

So here we are—the Great Flood. Sitchin says that the Anunnaki knew the flood was coming, and so they got into their spaceships and

watched the earth flood from the sky. They watched the devastation such a catastrophe can cause, and man was going to be extinct from the earth.

It was Enki who told Ziusudra (Noah) to build a vessel big enough to carry the animals and his family to be saved, because a storm was coming.

Now the Anunnaki must start over and build new temples, pyramids, new spaceports for their survival. Everything was underwater, under mud, so they built new cities. Eridu would be the first to be rebuilt.

It was about 300,000 years ago Enki and Ninmah created primitive workers through genetic manipulation of ape-women. The creations took over the manual chores of the Anunnaki. Enlil brings primitive workers to the Edin of Mesopotamia.

After the Great Flood, many of the survivors, even the Anunnaki, built their homes on the mountaintops because not all land was dry from the flood. This could explain why we see so many ancient cities high in the mountains such as Machu Picchu, Peru, and many others.

This would explain how in Egyptian mythology, the great god Ra, also known as Marduk, came from the primordial waters of Nun. Nun existed in every particle of water and formed the source of the Nile River. In other myths, we read about the first eight gods that created Egypt, four men and four women, that would also go with the flood. There was a pair of each sex in the ark/vessel. It is said that they came with stories of a much more populated earth, and if they were Anunnaki or any type of a star being, they lived much longer than the ancient humans. They can outlive generations, thus making them godly.

If the biblical Adam and Eve were the first human beings, why are we different colors with different features? Could it be that the four gods and the four goddesses of Egypt were of different skin colors and facial features? We are only told we were punished with the change of tongue (different languages), not our skin color and features. There are many Egyptian mythologies about the creation of the world, life, and the universe, as there are in so many other ancient cultures.

The difficult part is, What is myth? What is truth? And which ones do you believe? Even one Egyptian story suggests the earth will go back underwater at the end of the world.

Around 10,500 BC: The descendants of Ziusudra (biblical Noah) are given three regions of Egypt to rule. Ninurta, Enlil's son, dams the mountains and drains the rivers to make Mesopotamia livable. Enki reclaims the Great Nile Valley. The Sinai peninsula is had by the Annunaki for a post-diluvial spaceport. On Mount Moriah, a control center is established (what we know as Jerusalem today).

9780 BC: Ra, Enki's first son, splits Egypt between Osiris and Seth. This is not a good relationship. Seth ends up killing Osiris so he can rule all of Egypt. Horus, son of Osiris and Isis, will avenge his father's death, starting the first pyramid war.

8670 BC: A second war of the pyramids erupted. Ninurta empties the Great Pyramid of its technology and equipment. Ninmah has a peace conference. They divide earth from Ra/Marduck to Thoth, who will rule Egypt now. Heliopolis will be built as a beacon city.

Within a thousand years, demigods rule Egypt.

Now, we see more ancient cities that have withstood the test of time. The Anunnaki rebuilt Eridu and Nippur around 3800 BC. Civilization again begins in Sumer. Anu visits earth, at the city named in his honor, Uruk (Erech). In the end, he makes its temple the abode of his beloved granddaughter, Inanna/Ishtar.

The book *Ancient Egypt* by David P. Silverman gives a lot of information about Egypt. On page 116, under "Realms of Gods and Birds," it says, "The Egyptians saw the sky as the Gods' primary domain, although they could be associated with all regions of the cosmos. The Pyramid Texts tell of the time 'When the sky was split from the Earth and the Gods went to the sky.'"

Every ancient culture tells us the gods were walking among us on earth and would descend to the heavens almost at will. In many ancient cultures, they tell us the gods will return.

We cannot discuss the heavens and the cosmos without mentioning the moon and all its mysteries. There are so many different stories, such as it was intentionally placed there by the gods or a different type of extraterrestrial being. It is an alien base to keep a close eye on us, to watch our progress, and to make sure we don't blow up each other or the earth in a war. If something was to happen to earth, it would cause universal damage, destruction like a domino effect, maybe even to the aliens' own planet. If Nibiru travels in our solar system, it would make sense to protect this planet in order to protect theirs. Some believe the moon was a kind of space station, and that there are structures standing to this day. I have seen videos and read articles, but it's very hard to believe certain things on the Internet. But then again, some things are very unexplainable.

Sitchin suggests that the moon and earth were once one, and there was a galactic crash with one of Nibiru's moons and Tiamat. Tiamat was the name of earth millions and millions of years ago, before any life existed. From the crash, part of the earth turned into the moon, and what couldn't form became our asteroid belt. That makes the moon part of the earth.

We also have conspiracy theorists who believe man has never been to the moon, and it's been nothing but a great hoax put among us. But what we do have are plenty of reports from astronauts who have reported seeing UFOs in the skies, and even on our moon.

> Major Gordon Cooper: One of the original Mercury Astronauts and the last American to fly in space alone. On May 15, 1963 he shot into space in a Mercury capsule for a 22 orbit journey around the world, During the final orbit, Major Cooper told the tracking station at Muchea (near Perth Australia) that he could see a glowing, greenish object ahead of him quickly approaching his capsule. The UFO was real and solid, because it was picked up by Muchea's tracking radar. Cooper's sighting was reported by the National Broadcast Company, which was covering the flight step by step, but when Cooper landed, reporters were told that they would not be allowed to question him about the UFO sighting.

Major Cooper was a firm believer in UFO's. Ten years earlier, in 1951 he had sighted a UFO while piloting an F-86 Sabrejet over Western Germany. They were metallic, saucer-shaped discs at considerable altitude and could out-maneuver all American fighter planes. Major Cooper also testified before the United Nations: "I believe that these extra-terrestrial vehicles and their crews are visiting this planet from other planets ... most astronauts were reluctant to discuss UFO's." "I did have occasion in 1951 to have two days of observation of many flights of them, of different sizes, flying in fighter formation, generally from East to West of Europe."

And according to a taped interview by J. L. Ferrando, Major Cooper said: "For many years I have lived with a secret, in a secrecy imposed on all specialist in astronautics. I can now reveal that every day, in the USA, our radar instruments capture objects of form and composition unknown to us. And there are thousands of witness reports and a quantity of documents to prove this, but nobody wants to make them public. Why? Because authority is afraid that people may think of God knows what kind of horrible invaders. So the password still is: We have to avoid a panic by all means." "I was furthermore a witness to an extraordinary phenomenon, here on this planet Earth. It happened a few months ago in Florida. There I saw with my own eyes a defined area of ground being consumed by flames, with four indentions left by a flying object which had descended in the middle of the field. Beings had left the craft (there were other traces to prove this). They seemed to have studied topography, they had collected soil samples and, eventually, they returned to where they had come from, disappearing at enormous speed ... I happen to know that authority did just about everything to keep this incident from the press and TV, in fear of a panicky reaction from the public."

Read also: "Pioneering Astronaut Sees UFO," "Area 51 and Gordon Cooper's Confiscated Camera," and "No Mercury UFO."

Donald Slayton: Slayton a Mercury astronaut revealed in an interview he had seen UFO's in 1951: "I was testing a P-51 fighter in Minneapolis when I spotted this object. I was at about 10,000 feet on a nice, bright sunny afternoon. I thought the object was a kite, then I realized that no kite is gonna fly that high. As I got closer it looked like a weather balloon, grey and about three feet in diameter. But as soon as I got behind the darn thing it didn't look like a balloon anymore. It looked like a saucer, a disc. About the same time, I realized that it was suddenly going away from me—and there I was, running at about 300 miles per hour. I tracked it for a little way, and then all of a sudden the damn thing just took off. It pulled about a 45 degree climbing turn and accelerated and just flat disappeared."

Robert White: On July 17, 1962 Major Robert White reported a UFO during his fifty-eight mile high flight of an X-15. Major White reported: "I have no idea what it could be. It was grayish in color and about thirty to forty feet away."

Then according to a *Time Magazine* article, Major White exclaimed over the radio: "There ARE things out there! There absolutely is!"

Joseph A Walker: On May 11, 1962, NASA pilot Joseph Walker said that one of his tasks was to detect UFO's during his X-15 flights. He had filmed five or six UFO's during his record breaking fifty-mile-high flight in April, 1962. It was the second time he had filmed UFO's in flight. During a lecture at the Second National

Conference on the Peaceful Uses of Space Research in Seattle, Washington he said: "I don't feel like speculating about them. All I know is what appeared on the film which was developed after the flight." To date none of those films has been released to the public for viewing.

Eugene Cernan: Cernan was commander of Apollo 17. In a Los Angeles Times article in 1973 he said, about UFO's … "I've been asked (about UFOs) and I've said publicly I thought they (UFOs) were somebody else, some other civilization."

James Lovell and Frank Borman: In December 1965, Gemini astronauts Lovell and Borman also saw a UFO during their second orbit of their record breaking 14 day flight. Borman reported that he saw an un identified spacecraft some distance from their capsule. Gemini Control, at Cape Kennedy told him that he was seeing the final stage of their own Titan booster rocket. Borman confirmed that he could see the booster rocket all right, but that he could also see something completely different.

During James Lovell's flight on Gemini 7:

http://www.syti.net/UFOSightings.html

Lovell: Bogey at 10 o'clock high.
Capcom: This is Houston. Say again 7
Lovell: Said we have a bogey at 10 o'clock high.
Capcom: Gemini 7, is that the booster or is that an actual sighting?
Lovell: We have several … actual sighting.
Capcom: Estimated distance or size?
Lovell: We also have the booster in sight …

Neil Armstrong and Edwin (Buzz) Aldrin: According to the NASA Astronaut Neil Armstrong, the Aliens have a base on the moon and told us in no uncertain terms to get off and stay off the moon. According to un-confirmed reports, both Neil Armstrong and Edwin "Buzz" Aldrin saw UFO's shortly after that historic landing on the moon in Apollo 11 July 21st 1969. I remember hearing one of the astronauts refer to a "light" in or on a crater during the television transmission. According to a former NASA employee Otto Binder, unnamed radio hams with their own VHF receiving facilities that bypassed NASA's broadcasting outlets picked up the following exchange:

NASA: What's there? Mission Control calling Apollo 11 ...

Apollo11: These babies are huge, Sir! Enormous! OH MY GOD! You wouldn't believe it! I'm telling you there are spacecraft out there, lined up on the far side of the crater edge! They're on the moon watching us!

A certain professor, who wished to remain anonymous, was engaged in a discussion with Neil Armstrong during a NASA symposium.

Professor: What really happened out there with Apollo 11?

Armstrong: It was incredible, of course we had always known there was a possibility, the fact is, we were warned off! (by the Aliens). There was never any question then of a space station or a moon city.

Professor: How do you mean "warned off"?

Armstrong: I can't go into detail, except to say that their ships were far superior to ours both in size and technology—boy, were they big! And menacing! No, there is no question of a space station.

Professor: But NASA had other missions after Apollo 11?

Armstrong: Naturally-NASA was committed at that time, and couldn't risk panic on Earth. But it really was a quick scoop and back again.

According to a Dr. Vladimir Azhazha: "Neil Armstrong relayed the message to Mission Control that two large, mysterious objects were watching them after having landed near the moon module. But this message was never heard by the public—because NASA censored it."

According to a Dr. Aleksandr Kasantsev, Buzz Aldrin took color movie film of the UFO's from inside the module, and continued filming them after he and Armstrong went outside. Armstrong confirmed that the story was true but refused to go into further detail, beyond admitting that the CIA was behind the cover-up.

NASA has testified to a United Nations committee that one of the astronauts actually witnessed a UFO on the ground. If there is no secrecy, why has this sighting not been made public?

In July 1969, Apollo 11 land on the moon. During the broadcast of this historic event on the Canadian network coverage, they were discussing a light that kept appearing while astronauts were on the surface. Then it seemed to be dropped. One explanation for the halos seen around or near some of the Apollo astronauts was that it was gas being vented from their backpacks.

Timothy Good writes that HAM radio operators receiving the VHF signals directly picked up the following message, which was screened by NASA from the public.

Mission Control: What's there? MC calling Apollo 11.

Apollo 11: These babies are huge sir ... enormous ... oh, God, you wouldn't believe it! I'm telling you there are other space craft out there … lined up on the far side of the crater edge … they're on the moon watching us.

Timothy good uses "Saga UFO Special #3" as a source for this quote from the book *Celestial Raise* by Richard Watson (ASSK, 1987, pp. 147–148).

During transmission of the moon landing of Aldrin and Armstrong, who journeyed to the moon in an American spaceship.

Author Sam Pepper (otherwise unidentified and he has since vanished) gave this version of "the top secret tape transcript" from "a leak close to the top," as follows:

Moon: Those are giant things. No, no, no-this is not an optical illusion. NO one is going to believe this!

Houston: What … what … what the hell is happening? What's wrong with you?

Moon: They're here under the surface.

Houston: What's there? (muffled noise) Emission interrupted;interference control calling Apollo 11'

Moon: We saw some visitors. They were here for a while, observing the instruments

Houston: Repeat the last information!

Moon: I say that there were other spaceships. They're lined up in the other side of the crater!

Houston: Repeat, repeat!

Moon: Let us sound this orbita ... in 625 to 5 ... Automatic relay connected ... My hands are shaking so badly I can't do anything. Film it? God, if these damned cameras have picked up anything—what then?

Houston: Have you picked up anything?

Moon: I didn't have any film at hand. Three of the saucers or whatever they were that were ruining the film.

Houston: Control, control here. Are you on your way? What is the uproar with the UFO's over?

Moon: They've landed here. There they are and they're watching us.

Houston: The mirrors, the mirrors-have you set them up?

Moon: Yes, they're in the right place. But whoever made those spaceships surely can come tomorrow and remove them. Over and out.

When these transcripts came out.

In 1976, chief of the astronaut office Deke Slayton claimed that "I don't recall any of our astronauts ever reporting UFO's".

NASA claims that all photos, voice transcripts, all debriefings are in the public domain and are available to the news media ...

I suggest you read *The Day after Roswell*, by Colonel Philip J. Corso. He was a former Pentagon official, and he goes into great detail about the spaceship crash in July 1947 in Roswell, New Mexico, as well as how the military used the crashed spaceship to get reverse technology, dead alien bodies, and a survivor who was in the ship. But most important, he highlights what was not in the ship. He writes that the spaceship had no bathroom, water, or any type of food, meaning it looked like the spaceship was on a certain mission, just a quick look out on the New Mexico landscape, when something went wrong. Maybe it got hit by lightning and crashed. What is more intriguing is he suggested they had to have a mother ship somewhere because they did not have water, bathroom, or food, which one would need for galactic space travel.

Where were they going? Where were they coming from? Is the moon an alien space station? Or could they have an alien space station here on earth, somewhere where there were no men? It is an amazing book. He also writes in great detail what these beings looked like. He did feel they would be hostile against man, and that we must be ready for a not-so-pleasant encounter when they reveal themselves to us.

This brings up the topic of alien abductions. Thousands of reports are similar to each other. Are they probing and examining us to see how the Anunnaki creation has evolved? Are they still mixing their DNA with ours to make some kind of superhuman species? There have been many cases where women say they were pregnant and were taken back to a spaceship, and their babies were removed. Are all these similar reports another alien coincidence?

There are over six hundred people a day who go missing worldwide and will never be found. That's over 220,000 people a year who disappear off the face of the earth—no body, no evidence of foul play, just gone. In the last twenty years alone, there is an estimated 4.4 million people who have vanished! Where is the news media for this? It's breaking news if your favorite celebrity gets a divorce or breaks an ankle, but 220,000 people disappearing to never being found is not worth worrying the public. We are like sheep to television: they tell us what to think, whom to love, and whom to hate. ?They tell us what they think is appropriate for us to know. The higher powers make sure to control everything you watch and what they want you to think. Is there an alien spaceship station on the moon? Are the people abducted being taken there so that aliens can do their tests and research on humans?

A NASA researcher named Robin Brett once stated, "It seems easier to explain the nonexistence of the moon than its existence."

On November 17, 2015, at UFOholic.com, there was an article titled "that's No Moon. It's an Alien Observatory Created to Keep an Eye on Us!"

> Alexander Shcerbakov and Mikhail Vasin published an article sometime in the 70's named "IS THE MOON THE CREATION OF ALIEN INTELLIGENCE?" In the article, they ask some very legitimate questions and expose known facts that defy any logical explanation. The surface of the moon, the only part that could be studied, contains minerals and is mostly made up of uncommonly hard matter.

> Samples retrieved from the moon have also been found to hold forged metal material, which couldn't have formed there or arrive by itself. Scientists found parts of highly processed Uranium that science has never been able to achieve via natural processes. They have also found traces of radioactive metals normally used to produce Plutonium on a large scale. This is all clear evidence that the moon is not as inactive as we're being led to believe.

Could we have different types of alien species living on the moon? If so, are the Anunnaki still present? Did they leave earth? What if they never did? Could they still control humanity from the shadows?

Given the years that they live, it is very possible that Enki, Enlil, Anu, Ninmah, their children, and their children's children are still alive. For some gods in ancient Mesopotamia, the Kings List does suggest long lives of thousands of years. It is a fascinating time we live in, and there are discoveries every day that make us question everything we know and everything we have been taught.

This ancient Babylonian and ancient Mesopotamian sculpture is at the Louvre, in Paris. Notice the elongated skull. Was this an Anunnaki god? You see many depictions like this. Or are they simply statues for décor, and we are looking into a much deeper meaning than what it was? Were these the first human and animal tests Enki and Ninmah did? Or were they gods (aliens) that could transform themselves into whatever they desired, being praised for walking on earth as gods?

Does ancient Mesopotamia have depicions of an Anunnaki? Some believe it's Gilgamesh. Notice his size compared to a lion. Is this a god-king? Gilgamesh was king of Uruk. He is considered to be two-thirds god and one-third man. He built great ziggurats, was godlike in body and mind, was immensely strong, and was very wise. Gilgamesh traveled to the edges of the world and learned about the days before the Great Flood. He learned many secrets of the gods, and he recorded them on stone tablets. His story is amazing.

On March 1, 2017, "Earliest Evidence of Life on Earth Found" was the article on BBC News. It was written by Pallab Ghosh, the science correspondent. This article was very interesting. Scientists have found tiny filaments, knobs, and tubes in Canadian rocks dated up to 4.28 billion years old. This research was also reported in the journal *Nature*. Mathew Dodd, who analyzed the structures at University College, London, claimed the discovery would shed new light on the origins of life. The fossil structures were encased in quartz layers in the so-called Nuvvuagittuq Supracrustal Belt (NSB). The NSB is a chunk of ancient ocean floor. It contains some of the oldest volcanic and sedimentary rocks known to science.

Dr. Dominic Papineau, also from UCL, discovered the fossils in Quebec. He thinks this kind of setting was very probably also the craddle for life-forms between 3.77 and 4.28 billion years ago (the upper and lower estimates for the NSB rocks). Part of the interest in ancient life is the implication it has for organisms elsewhere in the solar system. "These (NTB) organisms come from a time when we believe Mars had liquid water on it's surface and a similar atmosphere to Earth at that time," said Dodd. "So, if we have lifeforms originating and evolving on Earth at this time then we may very well have had life beginning on Mars."

Here we have another great discovery, but with every ancient question answered, a thousand more arise. We are living in a fascinating time! New planets, ancient life, temples, statues of the ancients being discovered, space programs with endless possibilities, and billions of worlds waiting to be discovered. We seem to be going in the right direction. Or have aliens already been found and the higher powers that run the world think it's not the right time to tell us?

If humans were nothing but slaves, genetically enhanced beings to do labor, why don't they show themselves? Is there a higher, more meaningful reason as to why we are kept in the dark? Or is it as simple as profit? Someone always gets rich out of the ignorance of another. Certain powers around the globe count on your fears to stay alive.

We must educate ourselves and question evrything we read, starting from childhood. I think about the silly things I was bred to believe. I would get in trouble for asking questions they couldn't answer, so I searched for myself and found endless worlds, galaxies, and gods. I had an endless imagination of what can be. Some history books need to be rewritten, and it all starts with us. Read and then question everything you have read. Do your own research. My love for ancient history has me asking more questions today than ever before. We must read these acient texts with an open mind in order to search for the truth. Learn about our true origins no matter how uncomfortable it gets.

I read once that a candle loses nothing by lighting another. I don't know who was quoted as saying that, but it holds meaning to me. I am not a historian, archaeologist, or scientist. I have a million more questions than I do answers. What I do bring is a passion to understand ancient history, our past, our true origins, and our true history. Religion and science give us opposite opinions—and many times unsatisfactory or very poorly translated truths. It's hard to know what to believe at times. In the long run, it's up to every individual as to what conclusion or reality one wants to believe. I say as long as it makes you a better person, go with that. Ancient history, the gods, the myths, and the stories are a great way to open the mind, to imagine the unimaginable, and to imagine the possibilities of what an endless universe can hold. So far they have discovered about thirty thousand ancient Mesopotamian tablets, and most are translated. What else lies underneath the sand, waiting to be discovered?

SOURCES

Zecharia Sitchin: *The 12ᵗʰ Planet (The Earth Chronicles), The Wars of Gods and Men*

George Smith: *The Chaldean Account of Genesis*

Sir Austin Henry Layard: *The Monuments of Nineveh*

Micheal Tellinger: *African Temples of the Anunnaki, Slave Species of the Gods*

Donna Jo Napoli: *Treasury of Egyptian Mythology*

Dr. Ogden Goelet Jr., Dr. Raymond O. Faulkner, Carol A. R. Andrews, J. Daniel Gunther, James Wasserman: *The Egyptian Book of the Dead, the Book of Going Forth by Day: The Complete Papyrus of Ani*

David P. Silverman (general editor): *Ancient Egypt*

Kevin Burns, producer, *Ancient Aliens* TV series: *Ancient Aliens: The Official Companion Book*

Erich Von Daniken: *Chariots of the Gods*

Col. Philip J. Corso (retired), with William J. Birnes: *The Day after Roswell*

Chris H. Hardy, PhD: *DNA of the Gods: The Anunnaki Creation of Eve and the Alien Battle for Humanity*

Ancientcode.com

Ancient Origins

Printed in the United States
By Bookmasters